Little Red Cuttlefish

by Henry, Josh, and Harrison Herz

Illustrated by Kate Gotfredson

PELICAN PUBLISHING COMPANY

GRETNA 2016

The word "Pelican" and the depiction of a pelican are
trademarks of Pelican Publishing Company, Inc., and are
registered in the U.S. Patent and Trademark Office.

ISBN 9781455621460
E-book ISBN 9781455621477

Printed in Malaysia
Published by Pelican Publishing Company, Inc.
1000 Burmaster Street, Gretna, Louisiana 70053

With thanks to Alexander Von Humboldt,
my parents, and the Author of all things

A delicious smell drifted
past Little Red Cuttlefish.

"Crab cakes?
My favorite!"

"Grandma's favorite, too," said her mother. "Be a dear and take some to her. But stay out of the seaweed, and don't ink strangers."

Visiting Grandma is always fun, thought Little Red. And she bakes the best krill cookies.

"Whatcha got there?" asked a
sea cucumber.

"Crab cakes. For my grandma, not *you*."

Little Red chased the occasional shrimp, just for fun. "Wheeee!"

An octopus asked, "What smells so good?"
"Hands off! These are for Grandma."

"Special delivery—homemade crab cakes."

"How sweet of you!" said Grandma. "I'm not the crab-catcher I once was."

"I hope you both taste sweet!" roared a tiger shark, charging at Grandma.

Grandma scooted into a crack
in the coral.

"Leave Grandma alone!" said Little Red, nipping the shark's tail.

Little Red darted left. She darted right.

Too big to make a sharp turn after her, the shark scraped his nose on the coral. "Arrrrgh!"

The shark searched up and down and all around.
"Hiding won't help. I'll sniff you out."
"Go pick on someone your own size," taunted Little Red.

The shark tore through tube sponges.

He crashed through staghorn coral.

The shark almost had her.

Little Red squirted
an ink cloud and veered
right. The shark barreled
straight into a cave. He
wriggled and thrashed.

Little Red nipped the shark's tail for good measure. Then she darted back to Grandma. "My, what a brave little cuttlefish you are," said Grandma.

Little Red blushed even redder.

"All this swimming has made me so hungry," she said, "I bet we could *wolf* down these crab cakes."

And they did just that . . . along with some of Grandma's yummy krill cookies.

AUTHOR'S NOTE

Cuttlefish

Cuttlefish aren't fish at all. They are members of a class of animals that includes squids, octopuses, and nautiluses. They have a porous shell inside their bodies, called a cuttlebone, which is used to control their buoyancy.

Male cuttlefish have eight arms and two tentacles. Female cuttlefish have only six arms and two tentacles. The arms and tentacles have suckers for grabbing prey. And if that isn't strange enough, their blood is greenish blue.

Cuttlefish have an amazing ability to quickly change the color, pattern, and texture of their skin. They can use this camouflage to sneak up on their prey, which consists mostly of crabs, fish, and krill (small shellfish). Catching food is very important, because unlike people, cuttlefish never stop growing.

The cuttlefish's ability to quickly change color also helps it avoid being hunted by sharks, dolphins, seals, and other predators. If camouflage doesn't work and it is spotted by a predator, a cuttlefish can squirt out a cloud of brown ink to help it hide.

Tiger Shark

The tiger shark is a fierce predator that can grow to lengths over sixteen feet. It has five gill slits on either side of its body and not one but two dorsal fins. It has dark stripes that give the tiger shark its name, although those fade with age.

The tiger shark's skin can be blue, light green, or beige, with a white or light yellow underbelly. This is a simple form of camouflage because when viewed from above, the darker skin blends in with the darker water. When viewed from below, the shark's underside blends in with the lighter, sun-illuminated water.

Tiger sharks prefer to hunt by themselves at night. They are often found close to shore in tropical and subtropical waters. Tiger sharks have a good sense of smell and are capable of detecting the faint electric fields given off by living animals. They also have an organ along their sides that detects the faint vibrations of swimming prey.

Online Resources

Want to learn more about the oceans and sea life? Here are some helpful online resources.

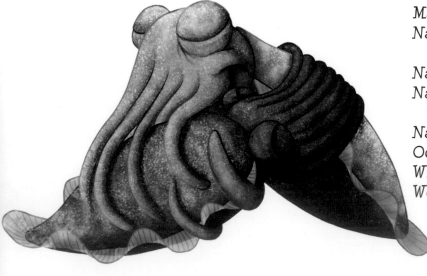

Animal Planet—www.animalplanet.com
Conservation International—www.conservation.org
Environmental Defense Fund—www.edf.org
Marine Bio—www.marinebio.org
National Geographic—www.ocean.
   nationalgeographic.com/ocean/
National Marine Life Center—www.nmlc.org
National Resources Defense Council—
   www.nrdc.org
Nature Conservancy—www.nature.org
Oceana—www.oceana.org
Wildlife Conservation Society—www.wcs.org
World Wildlife Fund—www.worldwildlife.org